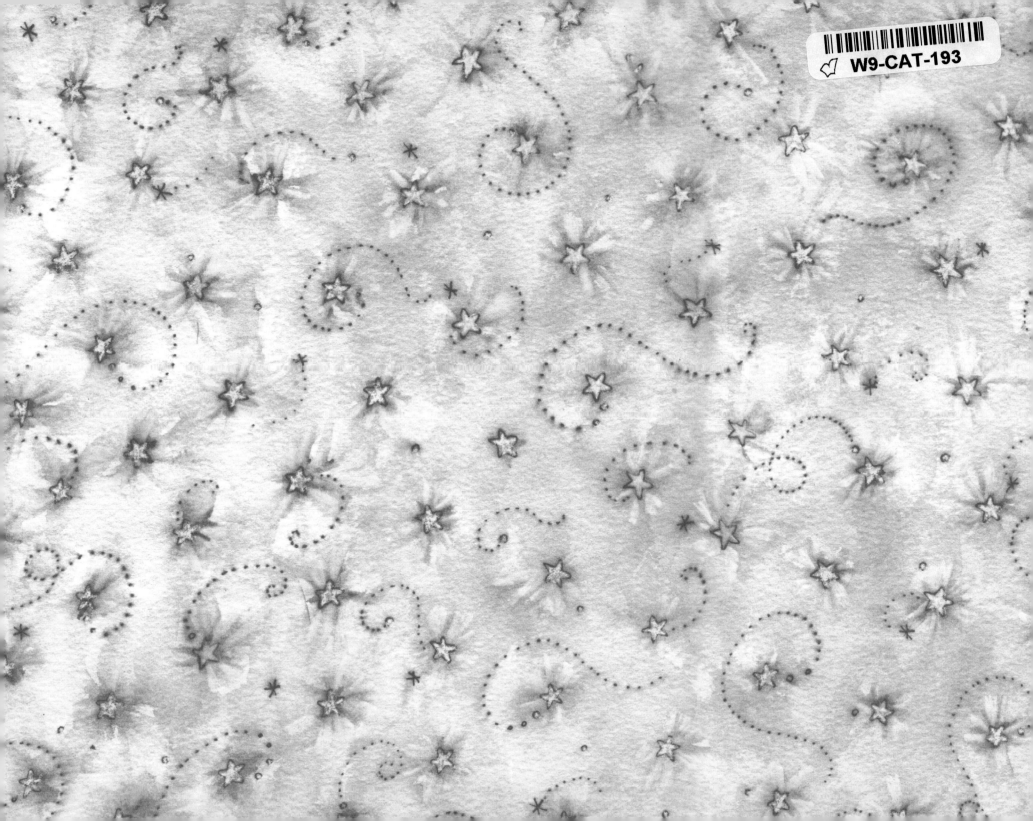

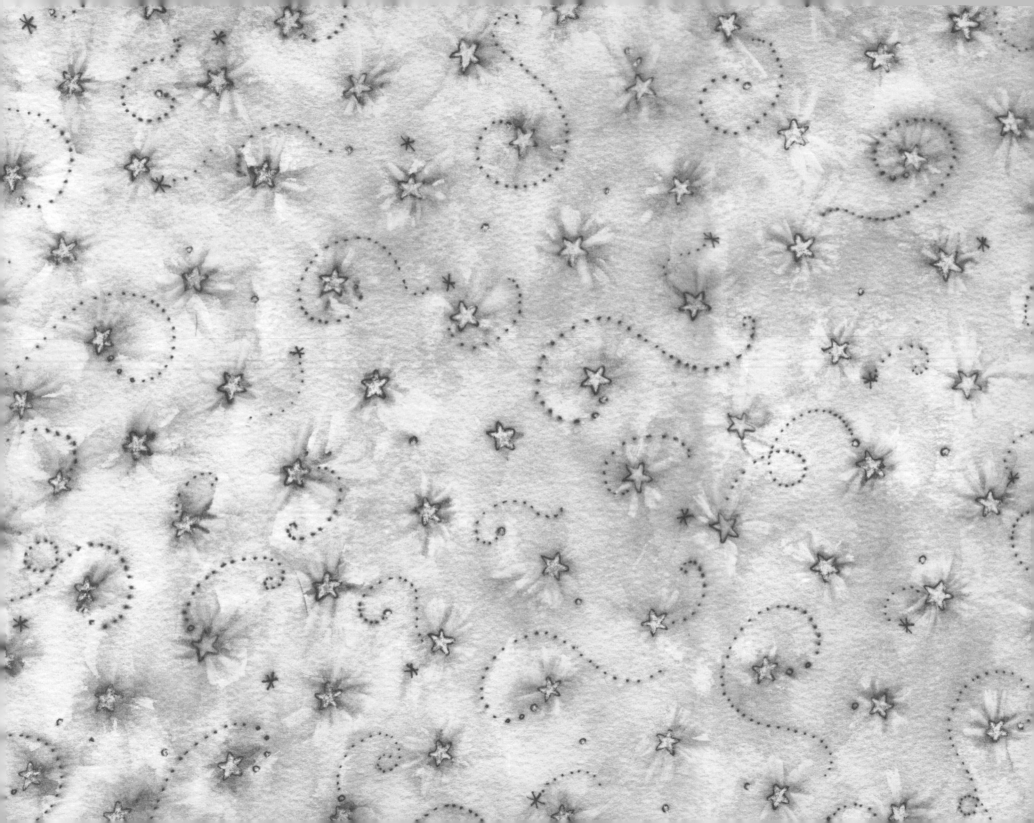

THE SOCK FAIRY

BOOK AND AUDIO CD

BY BOBBIE HINMAN

ILLUSTRATED BY KRISTI BRIDGEMAN

DESIGN AND LAYOUT BY JEFF URBANCIC

Always believe in fairies!
Keep reading!
Bobbie Hinman
2008

Best Fairy Books

www.bestfairybooks.com

The Sock Fairy

Copyright © 2008 Bobbie Hinman
Illustrations by Kristi Bridgeman, 2008 © CARCC, 2008

Voices on CD: Narrator, Bobbie Hinman; Vocalist, Michele Block; Pianist, Karen Campbell;
Bobbie's Grandchildren – Jacob, Ethan, Jesse, Jordan, Quinn, Emily, Jeremy, Kaitlyn, Justin, Lindsay

Text design and layout: Jeff Urbancic
Audio engineer: William Whiteford

Library of Congress Control Number: 2007907287

Publisher's Cataloging-in-Publication
(Provided by Quality Books, Inc.)

Hinman, Bobbie.
    The sock fairy / by Bobbie Hinman ; illustrated by Kristi Bridgeman.
    p. cm. + 1 sound disc (digital ; 4 3/4 in.)
    Includes compact disc.
    Compact disc: Narrator, Bobbie Hinman; vocalist, Michele Block;
pianist, Karen Campbell.
    SUMMARY: In this rhyming story, a playful fairy who sneaks into
children's homes is responsible for their missing and mismatched socks,
as well as the occasional holes in the toes.
    Audience: Ages 3-7.
    ISBN-13: 978-0-9786791-1-8
    ISBN-10: 0-9786791-1-3

    1. Fairies--Juvenile fiction. 2. Socks—Juvenile fiction.
[1. Fairies--Fiction. 2. Socks--Fiction. 3. Stories in rhyme.]
I. Bridgeman, Kristi, ill. II. Title.

PZ8.3.H5564Soc 2008   [E]
                    QBI07-600265

For information: www.bestfairybooks.com

This book is dedicated with love to all children who have ever lost their socks.
Soon you will know where they are!
And to my precious grandchildren - I hope your toes are always warm.

Ethan   Jacob   Lindsay   Emily   Jesse   Kaitlyn   Justin   Jordan   Quinn   Jeremy   Robyn   Laura

Do you believe in fairies who live all over the land?

Some are boys. Some are girls. If you believe, raise your hand.

Now, this may be true and maybe it's not.

It's about a cute fairy who likes socks a lot!

With his wand and his flashlight he comes to your house,

sneaking in quietly, just like a mouse.

You can close your door tightly, even lock all the locks…

but this little fairy will still find your socks.

With a tap of his wand - isn't it neat?

Like magic they fit on his head and his feet!

He mixes up socks.

He plays with them, too.

Gather 'round and I'll tell you...

what else he will do.

He tries on your socks, slides around on the soles,

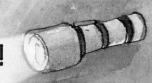

then pulls a few strings, and ZAP - there are holes!

Then he laughs and he laughs at your toes poking through.

Oh, he thinks it's so funny, but I wonder - do you?

Or, he may hide your socks.

Yes, this cute little fellow...

may leave you with just...

one blue and one yellow!

He picks up the socks that you left on the floor,

stuffs them into his pockets and heads out the door.

So, what does he do with them?

Where do they go?

Just look at his house and, my friends...

NOW YOU KNOW!

The Sock Fairy Song

(To the tune of Eensy Weensy Spider)

A tiny little fairy with a sock upon his head...
Sneaks into your house and peeks under your bed.
He picks up the socks that are lying on the floor,
Then he stuffs them in his pockets and looks around for more.

He loves to come and visit. He brings his friend the mouse.
With his wand and flashlight he looks around your house.
And when it's time to get dressed you open up your drawer,
But the socks that were there are not there any more.

And if you put your socks on and find they're full of holes,
Be sure to blame the fairy for sliding on the soles.
And now you know the secret. I really think it's true.
He thinks it's oh so funny, but I wonder, friends, do you?

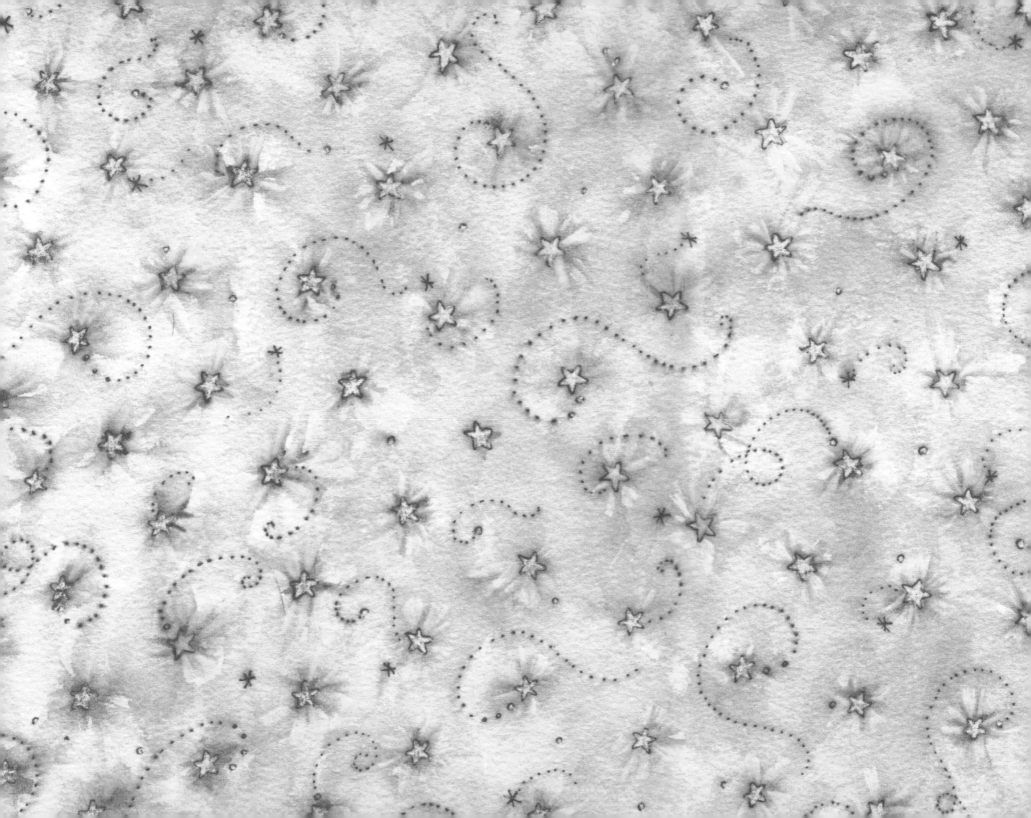

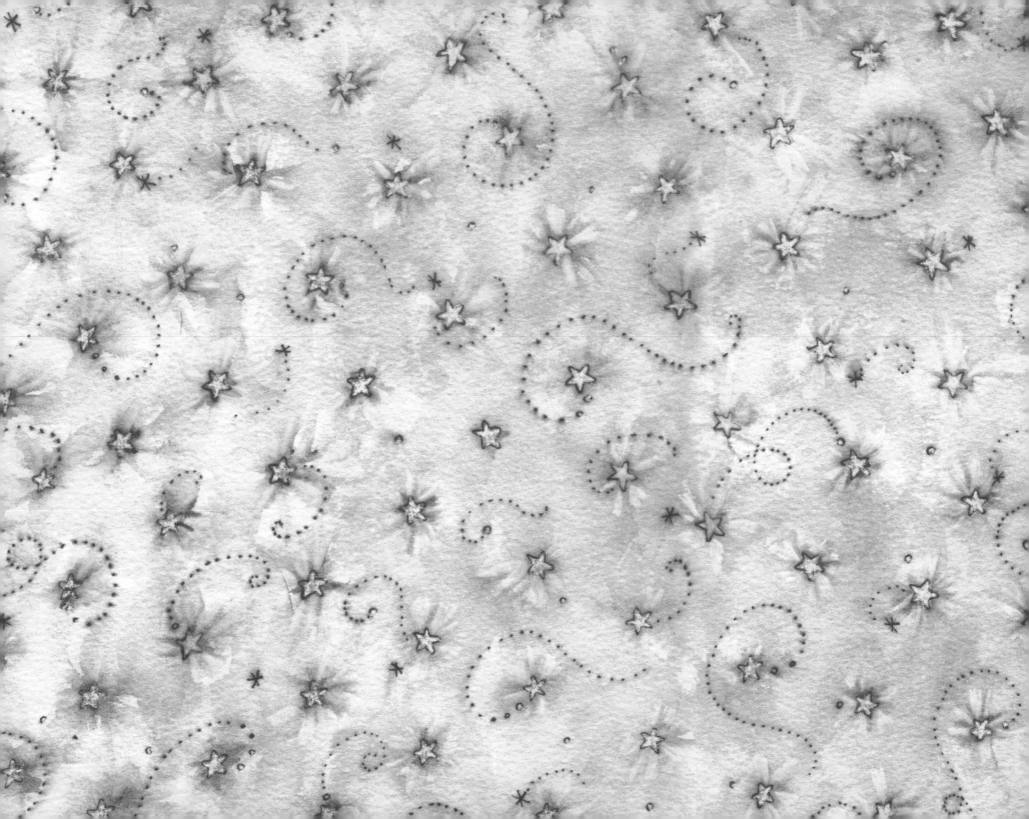